Chapter One

"Ssssh! Duck!" Spike hissed
frantically. They crouched as low as
they could in the short grass of the
clifftop. A small plump figure in a
pale yellow frilly swimsuit trotted
into view.

Primrose stopped, and cast her
eyes about. She was sure she had
heard something . . . Aha! Spike
attempted to cover the bright pink
spines on top of his head with a paw,
and let out a muffled "ouch".

Sometimes he wished he hadn't dyed them that colour: they caused a lot of problems one way and another. Mostly he quite enjoyed the effect they had on people. His parents loathed them. But Mole had dared him to do it, and Spike could never resist a dare.

Primrose yawned delicately and put a polite paw in front of her mouth. Sitting down carefully, she placed a bulging pink bag before her and opening a lunchbox set a table for four. "One for you, Moonbeam, one for Lovebeam," she murmured, addressing two fluffy toy caterpillary things. They were called LUV

GRUBS, and Primrose collected them, loving to comb their rainbow-coloured fur, and adoring their expressions of horrendous soppiness. "One for me, and one for –"

"What are you eating?" demanded Spike, popping up.

Primrose ignored her brother and turned to Mole, smiling sweetly. "Do have a toffee – look, that one is biggest."

Mole stretched out a paw, and Primrose gave it to him on a tiny plate, blushing.

"What about me?" protested Spike.

"You're not nice," answered Primrose. "You were 'sposed to look after me and you didn't, and I was very upset." She began to sniff. "Mole would've, I know, 'cos Mole's nice."

Mole, his mouth full of toffee, looked embarrassed. Since Spike and he had saved her from the clutches of a wicked fox, she had had some sort of "pash" on him and wouldn't leave him alone. As a guest of the

Hedgehog family, who were spending a week by the sea, he couldn't be too rude to Primrose. It was all rather difficult.

The rest of that morning was spent hanging around the beach near their guest-house, with Mole waiting on Primrose hand and foot.

"Pretty as a picture," smiled Mr

Hedgehog to his wife, as they surveyed the happy scene.

Primrose always seemed to have this effect on people, thought Spike miserably. He couldn't even have his ghetto-blaster on with his parents there. He picked it up and stalked off.

Mole watched helplessly as the black leather jacket disappeared crossly over the rocks and into the next bay. He wished and wished he could be with its owner.

"Be careful of Humans. And mind the tide," Mrs Hedgehog called.

But Spike had gone.

Some hours later the weather turned colder. A fresh breeze blew in from the sea, and a little wave splashed over Mr Hedgehog's toes. They decided to take their packed lunches inside. "Will you join us, or are you going to try and find Spike?" asked Mr Hedgehog. Mole, conscious of Primrose's eyes upon him, hesitated. "Er . . ."

But Mrs Hedgehog interrupted. "I'd rather he went after Spike. I'm a bit worried. These tides come up so fast . . ." Her voice trailed away.

"I'm sure he'll be all right," Mole reassured her. "But I'll go if you like."

Mrs Hedgehog nodded. "Come back in half an hour if you don't find him."

Two minutes later, Mole was trotting along the cliff path, two fat packets of sandwiches in his pockets.

With no sun on it, the sea looked grey and unfriendly. Mole looked at it with new respect. He increased his pace.

The cliff path wound in and out along the green clifftop. Every now and then, a signpost marked "beach" pointed downward. Mole stopped at

each one and peered over the cliff edge. No Spike. He noticed with a shock that the sea was much higher and still coming in fast. Mole began to run. He was really worried now. Another sign, another bay. Still no Spike.

Breathless, Mole had to slow down. This was lucky, for if he'd

been going faster, he wouldn't have
noticed the three broken twigs
arranged like this:

pointing to a
much smaller path leading
downward to a tiny cove. He began
to scramble down at once. Halfway
there he stopped, unable to go on.
Right below, black waves slapped
onto sharp rocks in a flurry of furious
foam. The cove was accessible only
at low tide. Looking across into it,
Mole saw nothing at first; then,
between waves, a flash of shocking

pink. What was it . . .? Could it be? Yes it was! Spike!

Spike was standing on a rock, as far out as he dared, gazing anxiously up at the cliff. He had put his ghetto-blaster on his head to protect it from the waves, which even now were swirling about his feet. He couldn't see Mole.

There wasn't a moment to lose. Looking along the bottom of the cliff, Mole saw a darkness, a hole. A cave perhaps? Probably it would be underwater at high tide; but it would give him time – maybe half an hour – to fetch help. He shouted, but the wind blew his voice away.

Mole thought hard: if he threw a stone, he might hurt Spike, or even

knock him into the water. He quickly
took a sandwich from the packet and
threw that. It hit Spike on the
shoulder. Startled, Spike looked
across. A great beam lit up his face.
Mole pointed, and gestured to the
cave. Then he began to run back up

the cliff as fast as he could. Would he have enough time to fetch help?

Suddenly he slipped; his hind paw was caught in a hole. But what was this: a crevice in the rock filled up with earth? Mole tossed away a few handfuls experimentally, and then some more. Lower down, the crevice widened out. A very slight smell of salt reached his nostrils. At last he knew what to do.

Mole dug and dug, scrabbling frantically with his strong, spadelike paws. He dug as he had never dug before, and as only a mole can. Down, down, down. And all the time he followed the scent of salt.

Chapter 2

Down below, in the cove, Spike summoned up all his courage and, hanging on to his ghetto-blaster like grim death, moved in to the overhanging cliff. It felt like walking into a trap, for there was no way out. Water sucked greedily at his feet, and once or twice he almost lost his balance.

The cave was quite a large one, but its walls were green and slimy: it was obvious that the tide came right in.

Spike shuddered, suddenly very, very frightened. He realized his feet felt cold, and looking down saw water lapping at his toes. Panicked, he ran to the back of the cave and flattened himself against the wall. How odd: wasn't that wood he could feel beneath his claws? A door?

Spike scrabbled round a bit and found no handle, but a length of rope. He gave this a sharp yank and to his surprise the door swung open on well-oiled hinges.

Inside was a further chamber, smaller than the last, and completely lined with deep, stone shelves. What could they be for, Spike wondered?

Suddenly he was knocked to the

ground by a fall of earth and small stones, and something warm and furry landed on top of him. A rather breathless voice gasped, "Spike, is that you?"

Mole had arrived.

They hugged one another in sheer joy and disbelief, and began to look about them.

"What a weird place!" exclaimed Mole, staring around the chamber. And all at once, Spike realized what the stone shelves were for – barrels. They were in an old smugglers' cave! Spike had read all about the smugglers of long ago. But this cave looked as if it had been used recently. What for?

He had scarcely told Mole his

thoughts when from outside came the unmistakable chug-chug of a motor boat.

"Humans!" whispered Mole.

"Smugglers?" wondered Spike.

The two animals shrank back into the shadows as big boots splashed through the water.

Spike curled into a ball as a torchlight flashed over him.

"OK, Sid," said a rough voice. "So what'm I to do?"

At that very moment, Mole heard a slight click and a gentle whirring noise close to him.

The two men jumped. The torchlight flashed round the cave again, and hovered over Spike.

"'Ere, wassat?" The first man

said, nervously. Spike trembled.

"It's only a bloomin' sea urchin. Now quit fussing about bleedin' wildlife and listen to me," said the second man. "This is what's going to happen. They'll all be taken off the *Lady of Columbia* at high tide tonight, and dumped here. You an' Nev pick 'em up. Use this boat so no one gets suspicious seeing some funny foreign vessel where it shouldn't be."

"An' you'll be in a lorry on the jetty? OK, Sid. Right on."

"Right on, Les."

The two men left. As their voices died away, Mole heard the soft click again, and looked up. "What was that?"

Spike's eyes were gleaming. "The click? That was my ghetto-blaster. You know what? I recorded the whole lot!"

"Recorded it? What for?"

"You'll see," said Spike, mysteriously. "Now let's get out of here."

It was a long hard climb, but at last they lay out in the soft grass on top of the cliff. Spike breathed in deeply and joyously. A hundred feet below, water slapped angrily into the cave.

"What was in that sandwich?" asked Spike, sitting up suddenly.

"Oh – um – snail paste."

Spike looked disappointed. "Any more?"

Mole opened the package carefully wrapped in last year's gossamer leaves. "Honey! And some crisps and some cake."

When this had been devoured, Spike leapt to his feet. "Before we go home, there's just one more thing we have to do . . ."

On the way to where the Hedgehog family was staying lay a human holiday settlement. Brightly coloured tents and curious houses on wheels sprawled over a green field. Humans of all shapes and sizes walked back and forth along a narrow lane leading to the beach.

Instead of avoiding this as they usually did, Spike headed straight for the settlement. Mole hung back in fear, but Spike pulled him along to where a bunch of ferns overhung the path. Several groups of humans passed, but no one noticed the two animals crouched low.

Then a little girl came by, all on her own. Spike stepped out boldly in front of her and handed her the cassette. Written on it in rather spidery writing, were these words: "Urjent. V. important. Pleese give to Poleece".

He bowed deeply, and stepped back into the shadows.

Back at "Ye Olde Smugglers Nooke Gueste House", Spike and Mole were in Big Trouble. Not only had

Mr and Mrs Hedgehog been terribly worried (and quite rightly so), but they were one and a half minutes late for the Evening Meal!

Mrs Sloeberry, the shrew who ran the establishment, was in a tizzy of righteous indignation. She had

known the Hedgehog family was a
Bad Lot (except perhaps for that
dear little girl) from the moment she
first saw that awful pink hair!

Unfortunately, just then, her
beady eyes spotted Spike and Mole's
dirty paws, unwashed in all the
hurry. She let out a thin scream, like
the nastiest sort of dentists' drill. Mr
and Mrs Hedgehog blushed to the
roots of their spines. The other guests
shrank into their greasy soup, glad it
wasn't them. Things might have
ended badly if it hadn't been for poor
Primrose who at that moment
chanced to choke on a fishbone.

Worried perhaps by the thought of
a death on her premises, Mrs
Sloeberry rushed over and thumped

Primrose on the back with a rolling
pin. Primrose was promptly sick on
the floor.

In all the ensuing fuss and bother,
Spike and Mole were able to finish
their supper in peace and slip up to
bed early. In this way they were able
to get in a decent bit of sleep before
the alarm woke them at a quarter to
midnight . . .

Chapter Three

Mole was dreaming. He dreamed of Primrose's LUV GRUB, Moonbeam, swollen to an enormous size, and with the face of Mrs Sloeberry. He knew that if he looked at her he would turn to stone.

"I love you!" she was saying, shaking him.

"Urk! Not that!" Mole moaned, turning away. But she was shaking him, shaking him.

"Mole! Wake up, Mole!" Spike was

saying, "Hurry up and get dressed."

Ten minutes later, a rather fuddled Mole was following a briskly trotting Spike along the cliff path.

A fullish moon cast sharp shadows, flashing and shifting over the sea. A little way out, the dark shape of a large seafaring boat could be seen drawing away from shore. It was the *Lady of Columbia*!

Down the tunnel they went, scrambling and sliding, until they landed with a bump on the floor of the cave.

All at once, strange noises rose up all around them. Screams, wild cries and groans; noises of terrible sadness and pain. The two friends clutched one another in horror. Gradually, the sounds died away to silence broken only by an occasional sigh. Time passed.

Slowly their eyes became used to the darkness. They could see that the cave was now lined with boxes from floor to ceiling, and they weren't just ordinary boxes, but cages. Cages filled to overflowing with birds of all shapes and sizes, and all colours of the rainbow. An enormous blue parrot was crammed into a cage that was far too small. It saw the two friends, and rapped out in a harsh, gutteral voice, "Quem é esta?"

"Er – English." Spike began.

"Ah! Eengleesh!" said the parrot. "'Allo! 'Allo! 'Allo!" It paused.

"Watter? No watter." It said in a

more desperate voice. "Wife – she seeck."

"I'm sorry, we don't have any water," Spike apologized. The parrot turned and murmured in a soothing tone to another parrot lying squashed at the back of the cage. Its leg was twisted up under it at a peculiar angle, its face turned to the wall. Everywhere they looked lay sick and dirty birds. None had food. None had water.

Just then, Spike heard a noise outside and the two friends quickly squeezed behind a cage. Was it the police? Cautiously, they peered out from their hiding place. Mole gasped. It wasn't the police. The smugglers were back early!

Spike was really worried now. Would the little girl have understood what to do? Would the police take action?

Minutes ticked by. The men were already loading cages onto the boat. Spike realized that if he didn't do something quickly, it would be too late: the birds would be gone.

Very quietly, Spike began to creep nearer the blue parrot. Mole saw the parrot bend his huge head down as Spike whispered something to him. The parrot nodded. Then suddenly, in a loud, commanding voice, it spoke: "RRRIGHT! STEEECK EM UP!" The men jumped into the air with fright. They peered nervously into the darkness to see who was talking. "ZEES EES DEE SHERRIF! The parrot bent down to Spike and muttered "O Quê? – Aah! Sim, sim! ZEE POLICE! Turn to zee wall and poot em UP!" it roared, really enjoying itself now. The men gave each other frightened looks and obeyed.

They were still like that when the police arrived three minutes later!

After a brief struggle, the men were arrested and taken away in handcuffs, shaking their heads in puzzlement.

One young detective sergeant was a keen ornithologist. She noticed the blue parrot immediately, and whistled, "Gosh! A Hyacinthine Macaw. There are fewer than 3,000 of these in the wild."

She looked around and shook her head sadly. "These are all very rare birds, and because of this, certain unscrupulous collectors will pay a lot of money to have them smuggled in illegally. Many of the birds die during the journey."

A gingery looking constable asked, "These don't look very healthy. Are they going to be all right?"

"I think so – even that one with a broken leg. Luckily, we found this lot in time. When they have recovered they'll be taken back and released into the Brazilian rainforest. That's where they belong."

As the blue parrot and his wife were carried away, the parrot managed to wink at Spike. "Obrigado amigo!" he said. "'Sanks, mate!"

"'S OK," whispered Spike, grinning. "Goodbye and – good luck!"

It was the following evening.

"I can't believe it!" exclaimed Mr Hedgehog in a voice which made Mrs Sloeberry, and all the residents of the "Smugglers Nooke" turn and stare. "We're proud of you son – and you too Mole." He held up a piece cut from a newspaper, and began to read aloud:

"'Tot in Mystery Hedgehog Bird Drama! Tiny tot Mandy Betts, 3, claims magic hedgehog gave micro-tape which revealed secret of multi-

million pound bird smuggling gang.
Police are mystified. '– Ha, ha!
That's got 'em hasn't it! Stupid old
humans! It was my son and his
friend that did it. Despite that
horrible hair of his, he's a good lad is
my son."

And the rest of the "Smugglers
Nooke" residents, including Mrs
Sloeberry, could only agree.

Under the table, Mole felt a small
paw slip into his large one. It was
Primrose. Spike caught his eye, and
smiling, whispered, "I'm afraid
you've really had it now. You're her
hero for life."